STONED TO]

SAYED H. ROHANI

Copyright 2020 by Sayed H. Rohani

All rights reserved

It was summer 2012. The garden trees were bent with ripe fruits. There was a variety of fruit trees. The sparrows kept chirping, and sometimes one was chasing the other. The dove was heard on an aspen, a little distant from the fruit trees. The fruits were falling down now and again, and there were a lot of them already on the ground, especially mulberries, which were the birds' favorite food. The garden was an acre large. On one corner of the garden, there was a platform, covered with carpets, where the people would sit, eat, and even the guests could sleep.

It was a hot summer afternoon. Though the weather was hot and uncomfortable, staying under the trees in the garden was restful because of enjoying both the shade and the fruit. There was a light breeze in the air, shaking the leaves.

Two men entered the garden from the gate. One was around 45 years old, whose name was Farhad, who was in his national dress. The other man, whose name was Noor, was 27 years old. He was sturdy and tall, with a lot of hair smoothly combed backward; bushy eyebrows, untouched and untrimmed; long nose; tan skin. He was wearing a pair of gray pants with a navy shirt. Although his shoes were old, he took care of them so meticulously that they appeared as new as in mint condition. He examined the garden from corner to corner and said, "You've a beautiful garden."

"It's Allah's bounty," Farhad said. "It just meets our needs, but not enough to make money out of it."

"That's a big relief. If you don't have this garden, you have to buy your fruit."

"True. When did you fill the position in the Parachinar checkpoint?"

"Three months ago."

"How do you like it?" Farhad asked.

"I'm on duty, no matter if it is here or somewhere else. I prefer the village—it is nice and quiet."

"And you are not under the direct supervision of your superiors. "

"I do my job properly, so I don't care if they monitor me."

"What have you been doing before this post?"

"This is my first job."

At this time, three people—Mahtab, Farhad's wife, 40; Deedar, his son, 10; Parr, her daughter, 19—entered the garden through the entrance connected to the Farhad's backyard. They were dressed in their own national dress. Mahtab was wearing trousers and kurta, with their veils. Parr was wearing a light blue veil, sprinkled with stars. Although her kurtah is countrified, it was shorter, newer, and stylish both in color and design. Her black hair, nicely combed, was long enough to cover her neck and shoulders. Her veil was transparent enough to make her hair visible. She was tall, with large eyes, medium nose, and attractive face. Her countrified dress was overshadowed by her beautiful features.

As soon as Farhad saw his family entering the garden, he said to his guest, " Excuse me for a minute. I have to go help them collect some berries to eat together."

"Brother Farhad, it's very kind of you. You don't have to bother yourself with it; I'm fine."

"It's no big deal," Farhad added and proceeded towards his family members to help."

Noor sat there on the bare carpet watching the garden strewn with fruit trees. On one corner of the garden, there were rows of aspens. He also caught a glimpse of Farhad and his family, but due to the distance he could not see them distinctly. If he had been able to cast a glance at Parr, he would have lost his heart.

Farhad climbed one of the most fruitful mulberry trees. The three others stood beneath the tree holding a drop cloth. Parr was holding one corner of the drop cloth, Deedar the other corner, and their mother Mahtab was holding the other two corners of it, holding it up in the air, spreading it out as much as they could to cover more space. They stood holding the drop cloth right under the branch upon which Farhad was standing up in the tree. He started to shake the branch with his feet. Mulberries started to fall on the cloth. Within a short time, they collected enough mulberries to suffice all of them, including the guest. Farhad climbed down, put the mulberries in a bucket of water, then filled a plate with mulberries, took it to his guest, and they both started eating rom the same plate. The rest took their share of mulberries and carried home with them.

Later that day, while Farhad and his guest were in the garden chatting, Parr entered the garden, approached them to announce something to her father. She had the same dress as before, and she looked attractive even without makeup. She appeared to be bashful and unassuming. As she approached her father, there was an exchange of glances between her and the guest. Though these glances were short, shy, and furtive, they were the most meaningful of all. They conveyed a great deal information to one another, and love was the theme and preamble of it. They were deep, deep enough to penetrate their heartstrings. They were so sharp that they had the acuity of glances of a hawk; so profound that they could encapsulate a book of information into a few words; so perceptive that they could decipher the most secretive heart. These glances informed that they loved each other, that they would be devoted and faithful to their love, that they would show a lot of fortitude and patience when confronting adversities. Besides being shy and unassuming, their glances proved ravenous. As both of them had little or no opportunities to enjoy such lovely exchange of looks, this one time opportunity was the best gift to take advantage of it.

She first greeted the guest, and then turned to her father and said, "Dad, Manan has come behind the door to see you."

"Why didn't you send your brother for me?"

"He wasn't home, so I came here instead to give you the news."

"That's fine," Farhad added, and after requesting his guest to excuse his absence, he stood and began to leave. Through his simple investigation about Parr's appearance before his guest he tried to show that his daughter's appearance before the guest was just incidental, and he would not approve of it.

When Parr accompanied her father to leave the guest, once again they exchanged their meaningful glances. This time their looks meant good-bye in the first place, and see you soon, in the second place. The two strangers left each other, but the impression their brief sighting and glances left behind was so tremendous and consequential that it rebuilt their entire mindset, creating such a passion and clamor in their lives that they encapsulated their total thoughts, imagination, and ways of life. In fact, love was the theme and preamble of this entire unanticipated situation. Love was born in a moment, and now it was trying to devour their entire time and thoughts and cares. This single moment was so significant that no such a moment had surfaced in their previous lives. Noor admitted that he was in love, though sudden and enigmatic it was. He felt he was in a precarious situation, not because he lacked determination and efforts. He was apprehensive of the circumstances that had surrounded the girl. He believed in himself. He was prepared to make all the sacrifices for his love. Parr was also in love, but she had not admitted that she was in love. She could not take it for granted, for it was too soon to be unwrapped from the wrap of tradition. She felt strange to love a stranger. However, she was so much impressed by the stranger that she was thinking of him all the time. She wished to see him again, and she was thinking of how to see him. Even she was thinking of certain ways to meet him. This love was not more than a tiny sparkle in her life, and now it was growing so fast that her entire existence was enveloped with it, and it was still growing and glowing by the passage of time.

Noor felt that his love was deep-seated, that he had to take care of it; otherwise, he was suffering like a thirsty or a hungry man. It was the first night of his love. He tried to sleep, tossing and turning, but to no avail. His thoughts were with Parr. The whole time she and her entire features were across his memory—her long hair, her big innocent black eyes, her nose, her beautiful mouth, and her calm and sober disposition. Her features were parading across his mind one after another.

Parr, likewise, spent most of the night thinking about Noor. Actually, she started to plan how to succeed to see him again, and she wanted to see him as soon as possible. She knew where he was working. She was thinking to visit his workplace, and if it were an opportune moment, she could see him and exchange few words with him. She knew they were both in love, and no misconception was conceivable in that meeting. She was thinking to see him, but she had not yet determined the time.

She was adrift in very enrapturing fancies. She fancied she became engaged with Noor, and his lips were touching her face. It was so delightful that she stayed for a good while with this fancy until she went to sleep

Parr made the most audacious attempt in her life for the first time. She never believed to make such an attempt, but, to her surprise, she had been reconciled to that. She decided to go to the checkpoint, where Noor was working, and if he were somewhere around outside, she would make his eyes pop out by her surprise visit. Her heart was beating; perhaps the beats were coming from her infatuation. It was absurd what she was after, but she had been forced to be reconciled to her temptation and accept it, and it was the first time that she had found herself confronted with such invisible force. It was quite a new experience, a new escapade, and a new audacity.

As soon as she arrived by the checkpoint, she chanced upon Noor, who was startled by her unexpected sight. Their hearts were beating, which resulted from surprise, delight, and their ebullient emotion.

"Hello, I'm delighted to meet you," Noor said with a rapturous smile.

"My name is Parr," She said. "I was passing by your checkpoint, and here you are…"

"Your name is as beautiful as the peacock's feathers (Parr means feather in Persian), and you're the most beautiful woman."

She was wearing her traditional dress but new—kurta and trousers—with a larger veil to cover at least her head and torso. Despite her previous day, she was wearing a little makeup, and her hair more stylish, which all this added to her beauty, captivating the man more than before. In order to save face, she told him that she was passing by the checkpoint, and therefore indicated that their visit was accidental. However, he grasped the whole truth and understood that she had come to see him. Therefore, there was no room to lose this opportunity inconsequentially. As a matter of fact, he wanted to take advantage of this time for his purpose as prudently as possible. That is why he started to praise her as the most beautiful woman to make known to her his feelings. That is, he notified her indirectly that she was his ideal woman. And now it was his turn to express himself briefly but wisely to impress her and help her form a correct idea of who he was.

"Your father is very hospitable. I had a very good time yesterday. Everything was amazing. You're an amazing woman."

"Where did you meet my father, and how did you know him?"

"A few days ago, my friend and I were in one of the town's restaurants to eat our lunches. Your father was also there. My friend knew your father, and thus we were acquainted. That day we all sat at a table and ordered lunch together. At one point we were talking about our past, and I came out with my own story explaining how my father had a garden, and how I enjoyed it. In the light of my story, your father mentions that he also has a garden with all varieties of fruits in it. Then he offered me to visit his garden one of these days to relive the spirit of the past. Your father also invited his friend, who is also my friend, but he was leaving the town and was not available. Therefore, the plan was made to meet your father yesterday afternoon in the garden for a summer fruit treat. And it was there that ah…" Noor stopped talking, trying to express his entire emotion, his heartfelt need, his ultimate desire, in that interjection, to open up his heart, to pour out his psychological craving, his thirst, and his hunger. The way he expressed this interjection was very unique, profound, decisive, laconic, and powerful. In fact, it was summarizing all his mental and emotive aspirations.

"You filled me with amazement," he continued after halting in mid-sentence, "with devotion, with fresh aspirations; you made me think of you, change my life, and start a new life."

She was listening to him with amazement. She wanted to be practical and discuss the main points, because they did not have time to lose. "Do you work in here?" she asked.

"Yes," he answered.

"Could you please wait here for a moment? I go take care of some business and come back shortly," he said and left. He spoke to one of his friends, and then returned to her, taking her to a corner, which was sheltered from the traffic, and there they could talk peacefully.

'"Where are you from?" she asked.

"District of Panjab," was his answer.

"What have you been doing before this job?"

"I was a student. Parr, let me explain to you: I have been brought up in a very good family. We were not rich, but we were very respectful and cultured. My father has a grocery store. What he earns is good enough to maintain the family decently. He taught me respect and decency. I'm very respectful, understanding, and humble. My father was marrying me to a girl, but I rejected his offer."

"Why?" she asked.

"Marriage needs a job, a nest-egg, or a shelter. I had none. How could I establish a family out of poverty and desperation? I waited to get a job, to build a little nest egg, and then look for a woman to get married."

"I respect your idea." she commented. "A lot of young people, without considering these points, start a family and make their lives and those of others miserable."

"You're right, Parr. I'm not one of those young people."

"And how do you evaluate your life now? Do you think you have reached your goal?"

"Though not thoroughly, but now I'm at least on the right track. I trust in God. I believe in myself, my efforts, my work, my struggle towards success and happiness. I can build an ideal family out of the resources that are available now. I'm quite optimistic that everything will be all right."

"I hope I am not a problem here for you," she said.

"Parr, you are a blessing! I'm so excited that I want to fly. Just wait. We have more important things to discuss."

He went inside. It was a simple construction with few rooms on the side of the street. She was left alone with a head of thoughts to discuss. Now that their intention was almost unconcealed, she felt comfortable to express herself and her position. He came back shortly and thus continued, "To save time and opportunity, I want to discuss my main point. You seem to be my ideal woman: allow me to express myself to you; allow me to express my love to you."

Although she had already violated her orthodox customs that she had come on her own feet to express her love to a stranger, she felt her burden much lighter when he went ahead of her and expressed his love first. She wanted to keep her modesty and keep her passion inside.

"I have a strong feeling that you're an honest man. My case is somewhat complicated."

"Ah, don't say that, it depends on us—our commitment, our determination, our choice. If we uphold our cause, we can pass the seven seas. Let me be simple and honest—I love you. I love you heart and soul. Trust me and trust in my love—my love is powerful enough to beat every single war, to leave all barriers behind, to pass all impasses. Explain your problem for me."

"A rich tribal chieftain has offered to take my hand in marriage."

"A rich tribal chieftain!" he expressed mockingly. "That rich tribal chieftain, I'm sure, is two times your age, with a big belly, smug and haughty, a mercenary little gold digger, or a roly-poly property owner—do you accept his hand?"

"No way," she said, shaking her head acrimoniously to show her disapproval.

"I'm also sure that you will not accept such an ugly hand."

"Absolutely. However, I have responsibility towards my father."

"You have responsibility, but you cannot kill yourself, turn a blind eye to all your wishes—to give sacrifices which do not please God. Please forget about it, and be yourself at the helm of your life."

"I will try."

"Not only try, but be determined and committed to your cause," he said.

"I have to go now."

"I'll make preparations to come to your house and officially propose. Once you're on my side, Leave all the rest to me. I have left behind both tough days and easy days, experienced different conditions, and I've seen dark side and bright side of life."

Parr considered her trip successful, but her cause was not free of barriers and ambiguity, which were triggered by her father. Noor's discussion was ringing in her mind, inducing her to love him more. Night was falling. The more the dark was spreading, the more she was putting her mind to him, as if there was a relationship between the depth of night and the memory of him. Perhaps, in the night there was less interruption, and she could pay undivided attention to her cause.

She was living on the second floor with her brother. Her room was opening to a terrace that was connected with the garden. The fruit trees were hanging on the edge of the terrace, which was protected with beautiful wood fencing. During summer, she would sleep on the terrace. Later that romantic night, she was lying on her bed, facing the sky, which was full of stars, with a full moon shining. She was looking at the stars, at the full moon, and at deep spaces. The full moon, the stars, and the placid night went so well with her romantic situation that a majestic combination was created, so that she was induced to conjure up a moment of love and romance. She found herself engaged with Noor. She was in a beautifully stylish green gown, with a red flower attached to its breast. Her hair, styled as a messy bun rolled up on her scalp, had added to her stature. An expensive tiara, engraved in precious stones, was displayed on the front of her hair. Her neck was decorated with a magnificent necklace made of pearls. Noor was dressed in black suit, his hair cut, his face cleanly shaved, and his eyebrows were neatly trimmed but still masculine. His eyes, decorated with kohl, looked darker, bigger, and brighter. She looked lustfully into his eyes, and he into hers. As she found herself engaged, she allowed him to entwine his fingers with hers. Then they lay entwined in each other's arms. She felt his hot lips on her face. Her heart started to beat hard, but she heard her partner's heart beating faster and louder. She felt so romantic, so excited as if she had used an aphrodisiac. In fact, she had turned an amalgam of things and perspectives into such a powerful love potion that by means of it the whole situation had become a reality. Her heart was beating, and she felt a tremor of passionate love running throughout her body.

Noor was more excited than Parr. For the first time, he was confronted with a dramatic change, a change he had never experienced before. No sooner had Parr left him than he felt himself confronted with an internal revolution. She was all the time across his mind—he was seeing nothing but her, hearing no voice but hers, and thinking of nobody but her. He spent the whole day like that. At night he enjoyed the same experiences as Parr did. The starry, moonlit night had added intense color and tone to his infatuation. His fancies were wild and exuberant. He was walking with her on a beautiful shore, in the moonlit night, their hands entwined, his mind full of her, his heart filled with her love, and his soul attracted to her. He was gazing at her, mouth agape with her beauty, fascinated by her face, overwhelmed with desire, whispering his love story in her ears. Now and again he was kissing her on the eyes, on the mouth, and on the cheeks. He felt so hot with his passion that he felt it was a summer afternoon, and he was on the beach bathed in sunshine. He fancied both she and he were lying together under the sun, on the beach, he in swim trunks, and she in bikini. He was enchanted by her pristine body that had not yet been seen or touched by anybody. He felt proud of her, proud that she only belonged to him. Her entire body was a tremendous fascination for him—her delightful ivory legs, her high-lifted breasts, her beautiful neck, her chin, her lips and mouth, her nose, her lovely eyes, her shapely eyebrows, her long hair. He was so spellbound that he only sufficed to look at her alluring body. Then he started to touch her. He felt himself filled with desire, an uncontrollable desire that almost drove him insane. He wanted to cry to her, expressing his love. He needed her help to get rid of this insanity. At this time he was startled by the barking of a dog. He left his fancies and suddenly came to his senses.

Now he started to think practically. He wanted to solve a certain problem that he had ahead. He was thinking of how to prepare to propose. He decided to do everything without delay because he considered his case very sensible and important. He felt that he depended upon Parr, and life seemed to be inconsequential without her. Therefore, he wanted to plan right and think properly to bring positive results.

He spent the night tossing and turning, while immersed in his fancies, his whimsical romances, his thoughts, his anticipations, and in his aspirations. Though he took great pleasure in his fancies and aspirations, he felt fatigued in the morning because of lack of sleep. The next day, he went to his work as usual, his heart set on Parr, his eyes riveted on her, and his mind totally absorbed in her. He was expecting to see her again, but with no success. The day ended and he departed.

At night he wrote the following letter to his father:

My dear respected Father,

By the blessings of God I am doing very well and hope you are as well.

Last month I filled the government post. I am satisfied with the job and am doing it successfully. I make sure to be economical to save some money to support you and have a nest egg for my future as well. As you have always aspired for me to establish my own family, and you have been searching for a suitable wife for me, I am pleased to share this happy news with you. I have found my ideal girl to marry. She is living in this town, where I work. She belongs to a respectful family. I know her father, who invited me to his garden for a fruit party. He seems to be a good man. Make preparations to come here for a marriage proposal. Once I am engaged, I can delay the wedding until I feel I am financially ready for it. You do not have to spend anything for me. I shall take care of my own expenses.

I want you to plan your trip here as soon as you can. As it is a happy event, the sooner we start it, the better.

May God bless you,
Noor

Once he wrote the letter, he folded it, put it inside an envelope, wrote both addresses on the envelope, and put it aside to send it the following day.

Twenty days later he received an answer, indicating that his parents were very happy with the news, and they had mentioned to meet their son within a couple of weeks. While he was fervently expecting to see Parr, their second meeting happened in three weeks. Although it was not such a long time, Noor considered it very long. This time, Parr was not as shy as before. She was more open and expressive.

"I was expecting to see you much sooner," he said.

"I want you to know that my father has tough restrictions on where I should be, where I should go, and what I should do. Right now if he knows that I am here with you, I'll be in a big trouble. Therefor, you should know my problem and do not expect from me more than what I can do."

"I understand your situation, Parr. But how can I convince my heart? I have my heart set on you. I see nothing but you, hear nothing but you, and feel nothing but you."

"I'm also trying to come up with a solution to fit our situation," she said, still trying to hide her heartstrings to show her modesty.

"Let me give you some good news—some time ago, I sent a letter to my father, mentioning about my relationship with you, and inviting my parents to start our engagement. Today I received their answer. They have informed to arrive anytime soon."

"That's a positive step," she said

"It's a serious business. I've taken it into my head to get it done. Everything seems to be fine and orderly. I'm sure things will go well."

"I hope so; however, who knows, things sometimes can get very ugly, too."

Noor stopped talking and started gazing at her. He found himself spellbound. He could not talk because he was overwhelmed by her love. She had perceived his situation. His eyes could explain everything. She looked into his eyes once, and then, out of modesty, she lowered her head, looking at the ground. She was calm and in control, examining her lover to measure the intensity of his infatuation and vulnerability. Along with this intriguing situation, he was also thinking about his fantasies he had entertained the night before. He put forward his hand to touch hers, but she retracted her hand as if it was burned. He came to his senses and realized his unexpected movement.

"I'm sorry," he apologized. "I'm just daydreaming."

"That's all right," she said. By what she saw, she understood that how much captivated he was.

That day they talked for a while and Parr departed. Once again, he was left alone with all his devastating thoughts.

A Few days later, Noor's parents arrived. Noor was very excited. He thought everything would be fine. They all discussed the marriage proposal and prepared themselves in terms of what to offer, what to say, how to dress, how to act, etc. As their discussion was presided by Noor, it was successful. All the important points were discussed, traditional and ritual aspects were reviewed and considered, and they were ready to propose. They spent the whole portion of the day talking about the proposal. At night their major topic of discussion was proposal. He was very excited and aspirant. His expectation was to the extent that he thought he was so close to success that he did not think of failure. That night when he was lying down on his bed on the terrace, he watched the moon and the stars. His romantic fancies once again crowded his mind. His engagement was consummated. She was wearing a sexy dress that he had prepared for her. She looked very beautiful in the dress. He could discover her beauty and enjoy it the way he wanted.

It was a moonlit night, and they were alone in the park, while the stars were twinkling. He was close to Parr, so close that he could kiss her whenever he wanted, without any disruption, any rejection. He was whispering his loving words to her, and she was smiling at him. He was looking at her charming legs, and when he was gazing at her half-displayed breasts, he felt enchanted. He went into a trance, as if intoxicated.

Despite Noor's and his parents' expectation, who were waiting for a win-win situation, their offer was rejected. It was a surprisingly devastating blow against Noor. However, he did not lose heart and hope because of a couple of reasons. First, he had Parr on his side, and he was waiting for her reaction against her parents' action. Second, he thought that the first marriage proposal is often rejected because they want to raise the value of their daughters both socially and financially. Socially, easy accession to a marriage proposal depreciates the girl. Thus, she is thought to be a cheap commodity.

Financially, if the parents expect money from the suitor, they reject the first marriage proposal to increase her dowry. Thus, Noor was entertaining these opinions; therefore, he still believed to win Parr's hand.

"What did exactly Parr's parents tell you when they rejected your offer of marriage.," Noor asked his parents.

"Her father said that he had pledged himself to deal with another suitor who had already made an offer of marriage."

"And what did you say to him?" Noor asked.

"I explained to him our good name and reputation, your good behavior and personality, your established job, and other related things, but he was stuck to his own point and did not seem to change his mind."

Noor was desperately waiting to see Parr and discuss the matter with her. He was wavering between sending his parents back for a second proposal or sending them back home and postponing the matter for later. Finally he decided to send his parents back home and wait for Parr to seek her opinion and see if she could offer some solution.

When Parr witnessed her father's rejection of proposal, she was more affected than Noor. Although she could not discuss the matter directly with her father, she did announce her concern to her mother, who told her husband about it, but it went unheard. There was no other thing to do about the proposal, and the only thing left was to defy her father, which would worsen the situation. Thus, she was looking for an appropriate situation to meet Noor and discuss the problem with him. A few weeks later she met Noor, who was counting hours.

"What a blessing that I see you here," he said.

"I must have a good reason to leave the house."

"Have you thought about the rejection?"

"Absolutely," she said with despondency.

"Do you have any solution?" he asked, his eyes lacking the previous shine.

"Nothing, seemingly."

"Have you thought of any plan?"

"Nothing yet. I'm puzzled."

"Have you defended yourself against this ideal—your choice to get married with your ideal person—an ideal, which is solely yours and directly affects your wish and happiness?"

"I discussed my concerns with my mother, making sure she would tell my father about my sense of frustration."

"That is a step that you've taken to let them know of your rights. But a better step will be to directly talk to your father and let him know that you're in charge of your life, that you've the right to marry whom you want, and that your wishes and happiness are involved."

"I can confront him and talk with him about all other issues except the issue of marriage, which is embarrassing for me."

"And that's the most important issue of your life, an issue that affects your entire life and happiness."

"Even with that, I feel embarrassed," she expressed.

"Parr, now your situation is quite different. Do you want to establish your life with me?"

"Yes," she responded.

"Are you satisfied with what you're doing?"

"I'm still thinking and looking for solution."

"Let me explain myself to you—I love you; my life will be a waste without you. Pleas take your life into consideration, be in charge of your life, and rescue your life and mine. There is no room for embarrassment. Our failure will be a tremendous frustration. You have to take a positive step in this issue, which is a definition of our happiness or misery."

"I shall do my best," she said.

"I'm also wondering why your father has rejected the offer."

"First, he's looking for a golden egg; second, I think, issue of Shia and Sunni matters to him."

"Ha! I will follow his religious denomination whatever if he accepts my offer. Who can be a better golden egg for you than me? If I see him, I can convince him about these issues. I think it is better to talk to him directly. Let me explain something to you. If there is such a situation that we cannot see each other, give your letter to Sarwar, who is an employee in this checkpoint, and he is a reliable man. You can also pick up my letters from him. Remember the name of the employee—Sarwar"

"I remember," she answered.

"Know your rights, respect your rights, and be defiant.

"But I have to act to improve the situation, not to make it worse."

"Your action will count."

They shortly left each other. The meeting was not as successful as Noor expected. He did not find Parr determined. Not that she was indifferent to him, or she did not love him, or her love was precarious. In fact, she was orthodox. She was not in a position to defy her father although her rights were in jeopardy. Although she was in favor of defending her rights, she still felt uncomfortable to challenge her father. Religious sectarianism was an important issue that could play a role between the two. Her denomination was very important to her; therefore, by no means she could change her position against it: she was voiceless against it.

Now that he was wondering he was taking distance from his ideal, he felt he was shouldering a bigger burden. He started to rethink the whole situation and take a different approach to drive his goal home. His first approach was to talk directly to Parr's father. They knew each other to some extent; therefore, Noor had no problem discussing things with him. However, Noor was sure of encountering a lot of differences to sort out between them. Noor explained to him: "I'm very well-behaved. I have always established good relations with all people who have dealt with me. I'm very kind. I hate the warmongers, the troublers. I'm also very honest. I've never coveted or stolen or attempted to steal people's property and money. Among other things, I'm a very hardworking man. I have always worked, tried to busy myself with something. I know that a lot of wrongdoing stems from idleness. Now let me explain to you that how wonderfully I may take care of my life partner: As I understand that my life partner is half of my life, I devote my full attention to her to live according to her expectations, to be happy, to be healthy, and to live in harmony and peace. I'm very kind, very generous, and very patient. She will enjoy me and appreciate my efforts as an educated, understanding, committed, conscious, and faithful partner.

"I understand you're a good person, but I have to honor my pledge that I've given to somebody else who asked for my daughter's hand before you."

"However, your daughter's wishes are very important and should be considered," I suggested. He did not like my comment. He considered it a pure intrusion into his daughter's affair, which he assumed a part of his family business, a confidence that no outsiders could touch upon or question it. Therefore, he responded with a change of tone, "As a matter of fact, that's my daughter's wishes."

"Absolutely," Noor confirmed, "I confirm what you said."

"I respect my daughter's wishes," Parr's father added.

Noor wanted to say something to repair his statement, but he could do nothing. He could not even comment on Farhad's deceptive statement, which he said he was "respecting his daughter's wishes." In fact, Noor could not comment on his daughter. If he did, it would betray his relationship with Parr, which was hidden from Farhad. Thus Noor's direct talk with Parr's father had miserably failed. He returned home with no success. Now he was moving into frustration, without knowing what to do and what to plan next. He was thinking about Parr and how to win her hand. The more he was thinking about her, the more he found himself distanced from her. The only thing left was to wait for Parr and listen to her initiation, to her story. However, he was sure no significant thing would come to pass. The story would be the same, and his frustration would deepen. However, her visit could make him happy, and now that was the only thing he wished for.

Sometime later he met with Parr, who said she defended her wishes, fighting for her rights and freedom to marry whoever she wanted. However, her exhortations, her cries, and her frustration got her nowhere. Jus as he expected, the situation was becoming worse. Parr's argument with her father has led him to suspect his daughter. When she was leaving the house, he followed her, finding her at the checkpoint, where Noor was working. This discovery led to more disappointment, restraining her freedom more than before. Parr tried to respond to her father's negativity aggressively, so that their relationship was affected a great deal, something that she had already predicted.

Parr's defiance of her father's behests not only jeopardized her relation with her father, but also Noor's relation with her father. From now on, she was under her father's surreptitious surveillance. She knew that her father was watching her everywhere she went, but she did not know that she was being watched more than what she expected. She could not meet Noor for months, and she desperately wanted to see him, even to the cost of her father's discovery of their meeting.

One afternoon, she decided to meet Noor. She left the house, went directly to checkpoint to see him. He was there. She seemed to be in a hurry.

"How wonderful to meet you, dear Parr, it has been such long time! I was searching for you in my dreams. The other day, I decided to come around your house if I could see you."

"That is an unexpected attempt," she said.

"Facing unreasonable behavior may create a lot of problems."

"That's true. A conflict between my father and me has already created problem. He's following me like a shadow. I poured out my concerns to him directly. I begged for his help, I sighed, I cried. He did not listen to me. He's very stubborn. Today I came here to let you know what I did, what happened, and what our future plan will be. It's better to make our situation clear."

"That's very wise of you," he said. At this point, as far as I think, we have left with one choice—to ignore your father and get married."

"That will damage our family reputation beyond repair. You know what that means in our tradition—that I've left my family as a whore."

"We have to sacrifice something to achieve something," Noor explained. "We cannot get everything at once."

"But this kind of sacrifice will be very undesirable."

"You will destroy your life to keep the tradition. I suggest if the tradition becomes so ugly, then you forget about it."

"We cannot forget about it."

"Though it is honored by time, not by reason necessarily. People are so into it that as if it is solidified by reason and wisdom. So what's your solution to our dilemma?"

"I keep showing my concern to my father by different ways. For example, first I'll appear to be upset and avoid talking to him. If he doesn't change, I'll appeal to harsher actions. For example, I'll stop eating, and still further…"

"I'm sure he won't concern himself with your distress. You want to kill yourself with your own hands.

You've already cried and showed your strongest emotion, but he has not paid any attention. You'll waste your time, and he'll push you into arms of someone that you'll have no choice but to accept. Then, it would be too late to repair the damage that has already been made. You have to burn and bear it."

"I'm expecting results from my plans. Our time is very limited for today. I have to leave any moment soon now. We have to discuss what is important."

"Don't forget that in case we could not see each other, deliver your mail to Sarwar. He's my confident. I shall also deliver my mail to him, and you can pick it up from him."

"Okay, that is important."

"If you could not see me, I'll come behind your door to meet you," he said humorously. She smiled.

"You're kidding. If my father sees you behind my door, he'll shoot you," she said with a smile.

"What is better than being killed in your way, for your love?" he said, smiling.

Until now their lives followed a spiral course, up or down. Thenceforth they seemed to be precipitated into a deep, steep precipice whereof, despite their efforts, they could not return back. Parr did carry out her plans to change her father. She felt angry and upset, stopped talking to her father, as far as she could. She stopped eating properly and regularly. Although she was eating some crumbs and nibbling at this or that to survive, she suffered from starvation so much so that she lost a lot of weight. Her father was watching her carefully, observing the changes in her, but he was not doing anything, as if he was absolutely right, and he was following the right path.

Her mother was very concerned about her. She expressed her concern to her husband several times but went unheard.

Parr could meet Noor a couple of times and they talked and confided their concern to each other, but they departed after a short meeting. One more time, Parr attempted to visit Noor. It was during that time that her father had suspected that she was leaving home to meet somebody. Chasing her, he found her at the checkpoint, where Noor was working. He regretted her action, approaching her indignantly and spoke: "You want to destroy my name and reputation. It is not worthy of you to visit a stranger. I shall take step to send him back to his town to forget about him…"

"Do I have the right to choose someone whom I value and wish to marry?" she asked.

"The way you've been acting recently, and the way you're solving your problem are showing your failure and proving that you're incapable of building your life."

"How have I failed while I have not yet started any project, father?"

"You know what you need: to stay home to save my reputation."

"That's the only thing you can teach me," she said, bursting into tears. That is the only way she could express her dilemma. She stopped talking, knowing that her words did not mean anything to him. He was doing whatever he wanted and decided whatever he wanted. She knew that her grandfather was like him. Therefore, he learned certain behavior from his father.

The following day, Farhad met with the tribal chief, filing a complaint against Noor, claiming that he was a threat to his daughter's chastity; thus, he indicated that his life in that town would damage the reputation of the town; therefore, Noor was concluded to be against the welfare of the people. Accordingly, it was requested that he should be replaced by somebody else. The complaint reached the headquarters of Noor's checkpoint. Soon he was dismissed from his job and was sent into the military service. One month later, Parr received the following letter:

Dearest Parr,

How are you, my love? How much your love is costly! I did not even peck you on the face, and I lost my job and was sent to the army. Your kiss might send me into the other world. Do you know what happened to me? I was accused to be a harmful person, a threat to the welfare of the people. God knows that I am a very decent man, and I have been no threat to anybody, anywhere, anytime. Have I been a threat to you? A lot of things are said and done in our daily lives that are not correct. I have no job, and I am not sure where my destiny will take me. It sounds that things are getting worse. However, I bear every hardship, but I cannot bear to lose you. I feel my life connected to you. You are half of my life. How can I live without you? Every moment you are across my mind. I see your face everywhere—when I look at the sun, the moon, the stars, the mountains, the hills, the trees, the rivers, the lakes, I see your face. I love you forever. I am determined to remain faithful to you. Write me as soon as you can. Stay in touch with me. Your connection is a great inspiration, great hope to look forward to.

I love you,
Noor

Parr learned that Noor lost his job and was sent to the Pakistani army before she received his letter. Actually, her mother, who had first heard the story from her husband, informed Parr of all this. While she was already distressed, what had happened to Noor multiplied her worry. She read the letter with a lot of interest and wrote the following:

Dear Noor,

I hope all is well with you. I received your letter. It is very unfortunate that you were dismissed from your job and sent to the military service. The whole thing has been against us. I have tried hard to convince my dad, but unfortunately, he has not yet been convinced. With all difficulties that I am facing and all the barriers in my way, I still look forward to meeting you and starting a new life. How is life in the army? I still hope that things get better.

Hoping for the best,
Parr

Three months past since Noor lost his job. He was expecting to get his job back, but to no avail. Not only he lost his job, but he was also sent to the Pakistan army to complete his military service. That was another blow that further distanced him from his goal. At one time, he found his goal so close that he could touch it, but, in the passage of time, it moved further away so that it almost disappeared. Five months later, Parr received the following letter:

Dearest Parr,

How are you doing? I am writing this letter from the military barracks. Will you be surprised? Do you think we are getting further and further away from each other? Who knows what will be next? Nobody knows about his own or her own destiny. Although we are a little distant from each other, our hearts and souls are close enough to feel each other's breaths and hear each other's heartbeats. The nature is gorgeous here: the sun, the moon, the stars, the mountains, the hills, the dales are beautiful. However, I find no pleasure in none of them. You are my pleasure, my heaven, my everything. Every moment you are in my mind. I have a picture of you in my memory every single time that I have seen you. Sometimes when I desperately miss you, I appeal to my fancies, conjuring up together a summer party beside a lake, giving me the freedom to kiss you, to hug you, and to walk hand in hand around the lake under the moon. Excuse my romantic language. Now these whims and fancies have become a part of my life. If wishes were horse, beggars would ride. Now I am a beggar, riding my fancy horses.

Do you know what I am doing here? After taking part in military drills, I, including all other soldiers, wait and wait to encounter an enemy, without knowing the enemy and their whereabouts. This is true of any other armies. They will wait for years and even for decades for an encounter: waiting in vain. If humans were honest and sincere to each other, life could be much easier.

Parr, I have some plans in my mind. I need your opinion about them. While I am a soldier, once in a while, I wish to come to Parachinar from Khurram to meet with you. These meetings will lead to our ultimate plan to elope. I know this is a tough decision, but we have been left with no other choices but this.

Please write me as soon as you can. Your letters give me hope and energy.
    I love you,
    Noor

While Noor was in the military, few more letters were exchanged between the two. As a soldier, he actively decided to contribute to the spirit of love, putting aside all indecision and reservations, and come up with a solid plan to succeed in winning Parr. A couple of times, he left his barracks and came to Parachinar to visit Parr. Although their meetings led to no sexual intercourse, they were seen together by the people who suspected that the couple had had an affair. He wrote a letter to Parr, explained his plan for eloping and waited for her answer. She wrote him back, saying that the plan was very risky and presumptuous. In return, she suggested that she would try to convince her father to let her choose her own husband. Noor accepted her offer reluctantly because he knew that nothing could change her father's mind. Despite this understanding, Noor had no choice but to patiently listen to her and wait for the result. The result was negative as he predicted. Farhad's negative and condescending attitude proved very daunting, persuading Parr to listen to Noor to carry out his plan, which was tremendously presumptuous: to elope.

Parr said nothing to her father; however, she warned her mother that her father's thoughtlessness and stubbornness would induce ugly consequences. Her mother told her father about Parr's warning. He did not change his position against his daughter; however, he was wary of her, surveying her behavior and business closely.

In the midst of all this, she wrote to Noor, informing him that she was approving of his plan; therefore, she wanted him to specify an elopement plan, indicating each and every step, the date, the time, the place, etc.

Noor wrote a letter in response to Parr, explaining his plan in details. He also included his cellphone number to contact him if she could. Their rendezvous was Noor's friend's home in Parachinar, capital of Khurram. The date, the time, and the address were all discretely enumerated. This was his last letter devoted to important information to help their plan to elope. Although his letter was void of romantic expressions, it had been prepared with a lot of excitement and fervor because it was defining their most crucial chapter of their relationship. It was short but very important.

As soon as Parr received the letter, she waned to provide herself with a cellphone to establish electronic communication with Noor. She knew it was the safest way to contact each other. She called him, and he was on the phone. They could talk anytime they wanted, and as they were in a distance, he could express his love freely, though she was still reserved and felt bashful. They did not change the time they were supposed to meet each other. They wanted to act according to their laid out plan. Noor was all smiles and full of exuberance. He thought he was a heartbeat away from success. His hope once again started to bloom. He enjoyed that kind of feeling when his parents first started to make a marriage proposal. Once again, in the light of this new plan, their dream started to burgeon, their imaginations grew wider and jollier, and their thoughts were inspired with vitality and stamina. Parr's thoughts and fancies were an amalgam of both pleasure and worry. Eloping meant a tremendous venture, a venture into the unknown, where it could be full of danger.

It was Monday afternoon. As the plan had already been made, and she had a good time to think about and make preparations, she was ready for the adventure, though it did not involve much preparation. What mostly she needed to carry was her cellphone, some money, some makeup, some light clothes, and other paraphernalia necessary for the escapade. When she saw nobody was around, she left the house and left for the rendezvous. She had to pass through the market place of the town to reach the place. She was swift, determined, and vigilant. She was in contact with Noor, and according to their calculation, they were to reach the designated place simultaneously, or perhaps one after another, with a little difference of time. He got there first, and then she followed him. Both of them had arrived there peacefully and uneventfully. For the first time, he kissed her on the cheek. Although feeling abashed, she showed no objection. He felt free to kiss her because he thought she was his. She had entrusted herself to him and accepted his love. He was convinced that his love was secure, and he was prepared for any sacrifice to protect her. They were so excited that they thought about nothing but success, prosperity, hearts and flowers. Her first kiss was the most precious gift in his life. He considered himself the happiest and luckiest creature in the world. He found himself in the paradise, among the stars, in the best state of mind, with the best spirit. He assumed to be the richest, the most comfortable man.

They had no time to waste. They had to go to reach their destination as soon as possible. He wanted to take her home, wed her officially, and to live together happily and proudly. While they were walking across the market place to have access to transportation to leave the town, they were accosted by a group of four militiamen.

"You are adulterators," one of the armed men, who seemed to be the head of the group, spoke patronizingly. "You have to be punished."

"We are not!" Noor defended.

"We are not!" Parr also defended, covering her face with her veil.

"Have you married?" inquired the group leader.

"We are going to marry," Noor added.

"How can you walk together and have a relationship like a husband and wife without marriage?"

"We're together to go to a mullah to officially wed us," Parr presented this idea to soften the situation.

"You're adulterators!" the armed man screamed at her. " First you have to get married and then walk together. We know that you have been together without being married officially, and now you are trying to run away together to involve yourselves in adultery freely. You have to be punished to set an example for those perpetrators who commit this capital crime."

Noor in the beginning appeared to be indifferent and calm towards the armed men, taking them lightly to hearten Parr and temper the situation. When Parr started to cry, he began to talk to the armed men with a serious tone, "We're innocent. You're accusing us of something that we haven't committed and have no intention to commit."

"We are not judges to decide your case right now," said the group leader. We are going to deliver both of you to the tribal chieftain to refer your case to the tribal court."

"Why should we go to the tribal chieftain in the first place?" Noor inquired. "We've done nothing. We're innocent."

"We're absolutely innocent," she said, crying softly. "We're going to the mosque to see the mullah to wed us Officially."

"You've already passed by the mosque," said the group leader. "You are running away from the town to enjoy a perfect romance. You've been having an affair for some good time. Adulterators, how can you fool us? March toward the tribal headquarter."

"But what's our wrongdoing?" Noor asked.

"You're accusing us of a something that we're innocent of," she said tearfully.

"March on!" the group leader threatened. "You have to pay the price. If you proved to be innocent, then you'll be freed without any charges."

The militiamen walked the two innocent couple into the tribal headquarters at gunpoints. Noor knew very well the danger they were confronted, but he did his best to be firm and tenacious to make the situation bearable and less serious. He knew that the tribal court decisions were more subjective than objective. The jury's decision was more emotionally motivated than intellectually corroborated. In the light of their previous verdicts and rulings, he expected horrible consequences. As soon as they arrived at the destination, Noor and Parr were separated and locked up as adulterators. Their case went to the tribal chieftain, who, seeing the seriousness of the matter, referred the case to the tribal court. The judge selected the tribal elders to determine the case.

Failing to consider the consequences of their behavior, flaunting their significance by taking pleasure in jeopardizing the lives of two innocent persons, the four militiamen proved an eminent threat, their accusations fulfilling, their rumors transforming into facts.

When the jury asked them about the two innocent people, they explained that they had been together for sometimes, and the last time they had been seen together inside a certain friend's house. The jury assumed—being seen together inside a friend's house—as a euphemism for having an affair. Therefore, their adultery was substantiated.

The following day, this verdict was announced. Noor should be stoned to death. Parr should be shot to death. Nobody could intervene with the verdict or question it because it was thought to be based on Quran. In truth, the Quran was violated two times by this verdict. First, there is nothing mentioned about stoning to death in Quran; second, the guilt or innocence of those who are accused of adultery should be determined by four witnesses who have seen them caught in adultery.

The following day most of the people in Parachinar knew of the fate of Noor and Parr. The verdict was carried out: Noor was stoned to death, and Parr was waiting with horror to be shot to death.

Sometime time keeps the tradition so high that even the strongest reason cannot reach it.

Printed in Great Britain
by Amazon